About the Author

Jacquelyne Lynn lives in Western Sydney with the real-life 'Graves'. She has always been creative and has an interest in anything that is weird and wonderful. She has a passion for creating art forms, from unusual sculptures to drawings, quirky and fun writing, horrifying things and making people squirm with disgust. She loves spooky dolls, especially Living Dead Dolls. Jackie completed a diploma in fine arts, majoring in ceramics and photography, and now works as a Dental Assistant, where she gets pleasure out of making her work colleagues laugh and particularly likes the dental lab where her creativity can come to life with all the plaster and creepy teeth. She loves nature, rainforests, cemeteries and Tim Burton characters, which she finds inspiring and helpful in sparking her imagination.

THE GRAVES

By

Jacquelyne Lynn

AUSTIN MACAULEY PUBLISHERS™
LONDON * CAMBRIDGE * NEW YORK * SHARJAH

Copyright © Jacquelyne Lynn (2018)

Ordering Information:
Quantity sales: special discounts are available on quantity purchases by corporations, associations, and others. For details, contact the publisher at the address below.

First Edition Published: 2018 (Austin Macauley Publishers™ LLC)

Jacquelyne Lynn
The Graves

ISBN 9781643783147 (Paperback)
ISBN 9781643783154 (Hardback)
ISBN 9781643783161 (E-Book)

The main category of the book — Juvenile Fiction / Ghost Stories
www.austinmacauley.com/us

Second Edition (2018)
Austin Macauley Publishers™ LLC
40 Wall Street, 28th Floor
New York, NY 10005
USA

mail-usa@austinmacauley.com
+1 (646) 5125767

Dedication

I dedicate this book to my wonderful husband, David and my children, Ashley, Billy and Steven.

Acknowledgement

I would like to acknowledge the help of my wonderful husband, David; my children, Ashley, Billy and Steven; my father, Jack or "Pop" and my beautiful mother, Barbara or "Nan". Without them, I would not have been inspired to create this book. I would also like to thank my brother, Dode, who always makes me hysterically laugh and also keeps me grounded and real. I would like to thank my friend, Samantha, who I can trust with my life and on whom I can always rely on for support. My friend, Sharna or "Maggot", who I read this story to and who encouraged me to send it in. She is a very supportive mate. I would also like to dedicate this book to the amazing, wonderful, and talented Tim Burton and the pleasure that I and my family have enjoyed over the years from his exceptional mind that brings amazing characters to life; he is a true inspiration. I would like to thank little Miss Katelyn (because I can!), and Austin Macauley Publishers and their illustrators for accepting my book and bringing it to life.

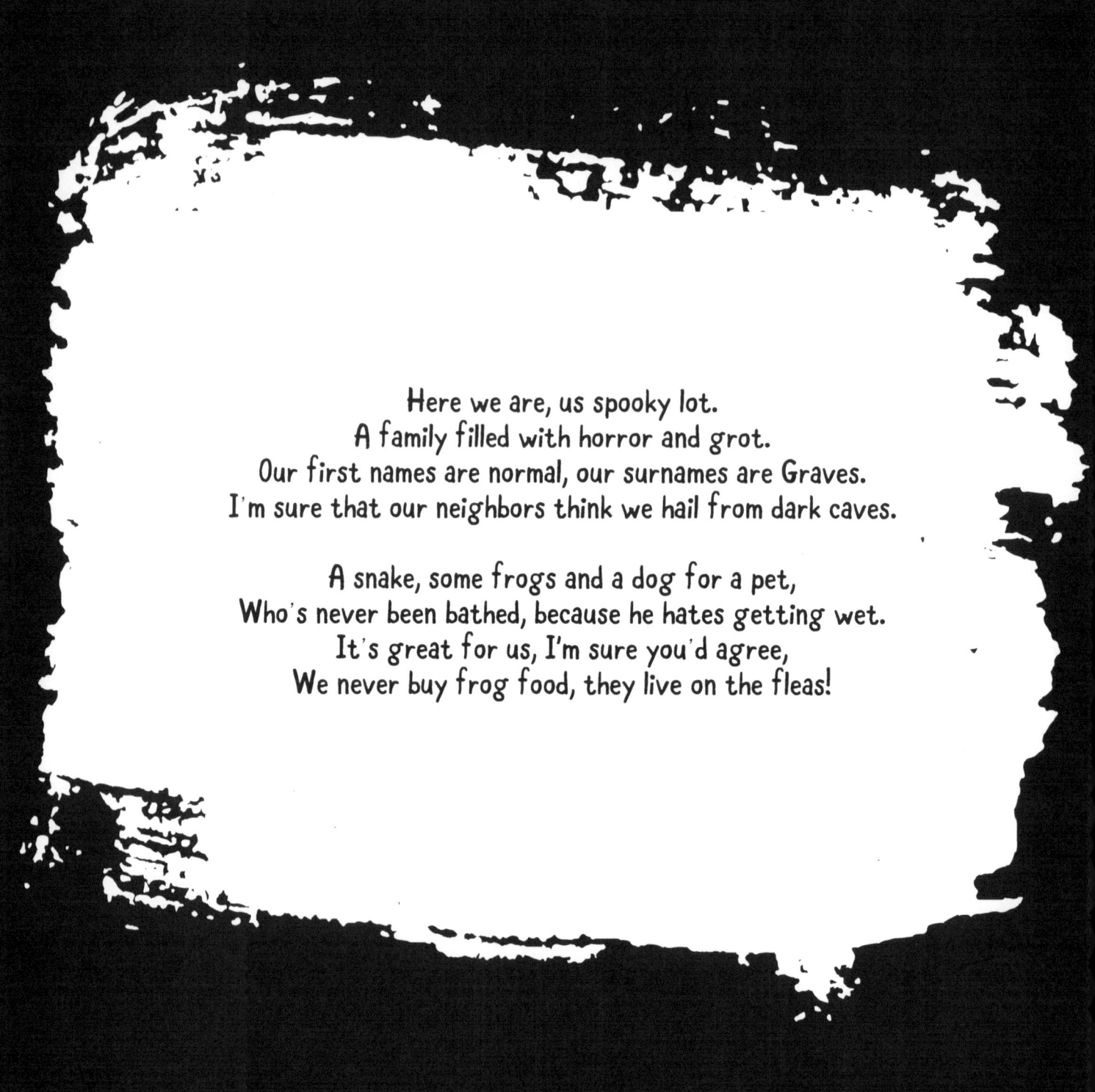

Here we are, us spooky lot.
A family filled with horror and grot.
Our first names are normal, our surnames are Graves.
I'm sure that our neighbors think we hail from dark caves.

A snake, some frogs and a dog for a pet,
Who's never been bathed, because he hates getting wet.
It's great for us, I'm sure you'd agree,
We never buy frog food, they live on the fleas!

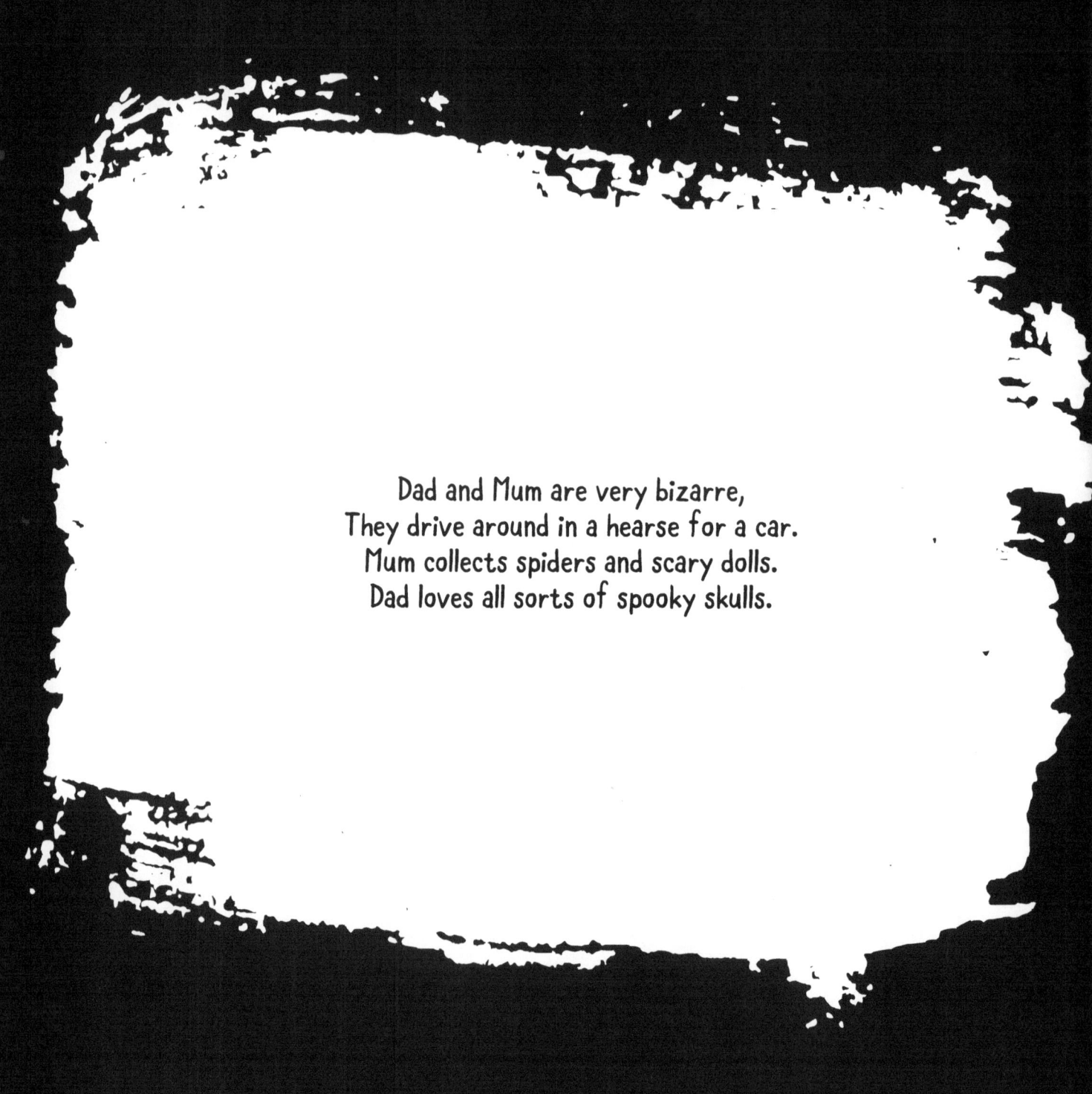

Dad and Mum are very bizarre,
They drive around in a hearse for a car.
Mum collects spiders and scary dolls.
Dad loves all sorts of spooky skulls.

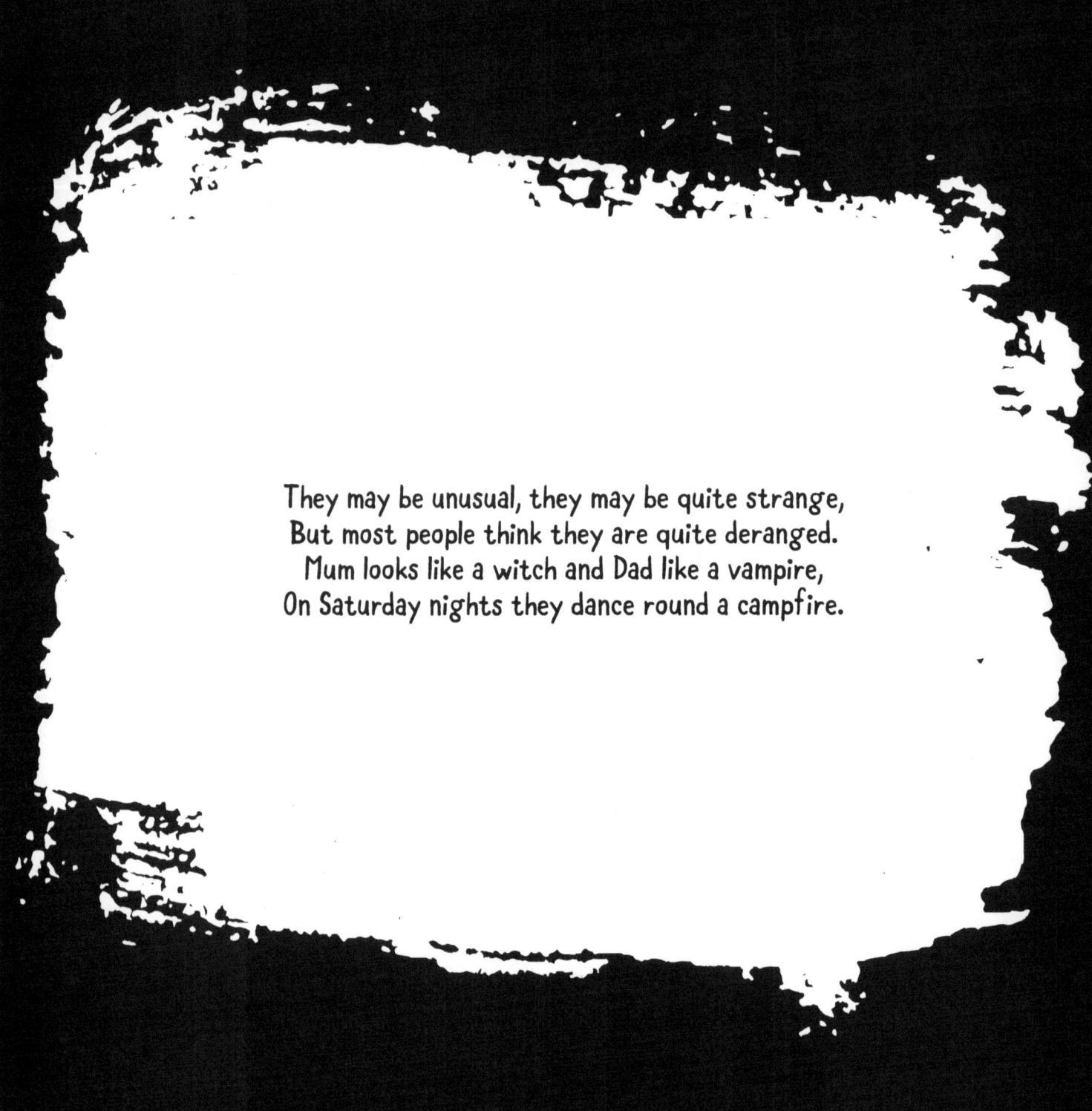

They may be unusual, they may be quite strange,
But most people think they are quite deranged.
Mum looks like a witch and Dad like a vampire,
On Saturday nights they dance round a campfire.

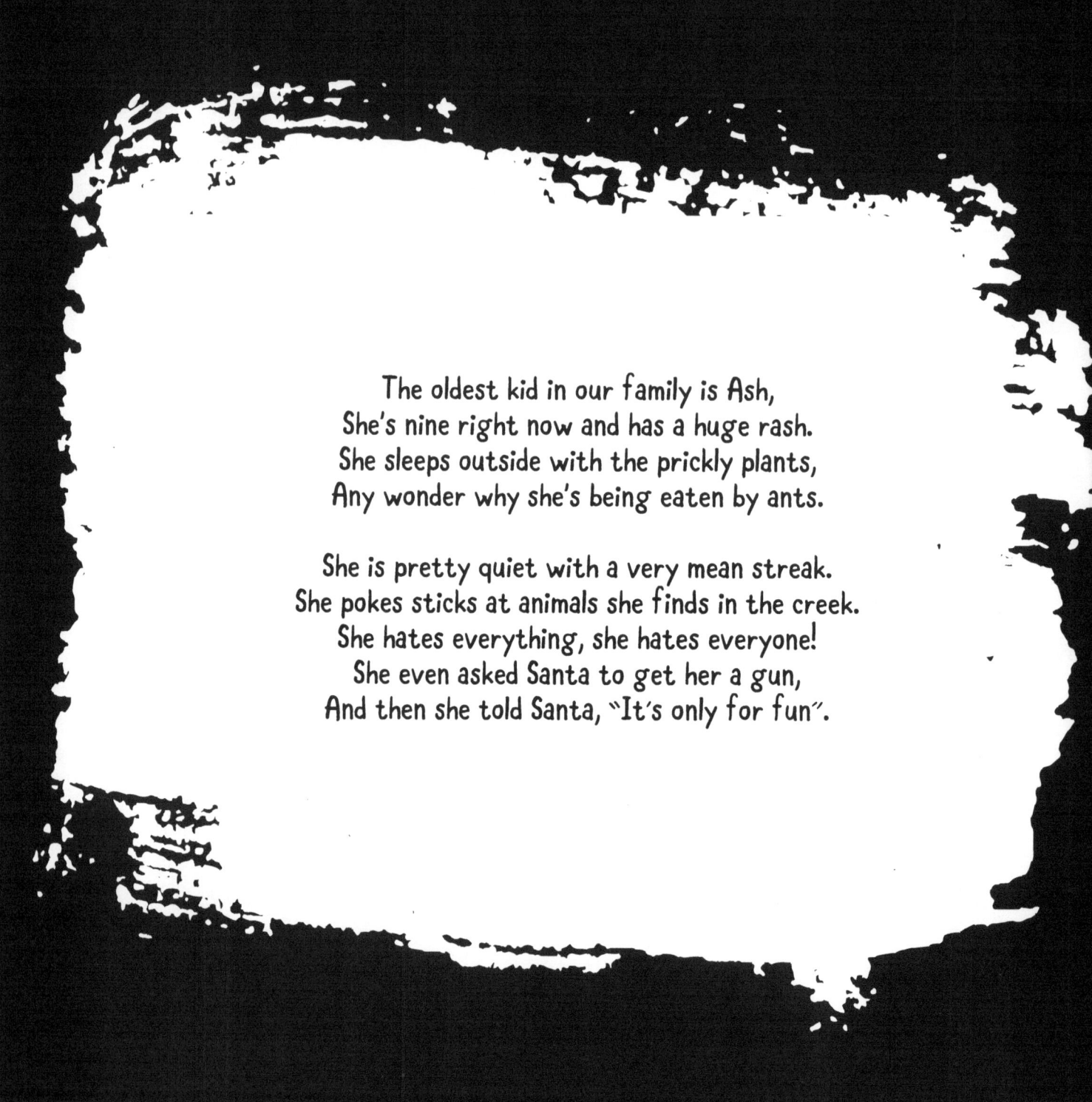

The oldest kid in our family is Ash,
She's nine right now and has a huge rash.
She sleeps outside with the prickly plants,
Any wonder why she's being eaten by ants.

She is pretty quiet with a very mean streak.
She pokes sticks at animals she finds in the creek.
She hates everything, she hates everyone!
She even asked Santa to get her a gun,
And then she told Santa, "It's only for fun".

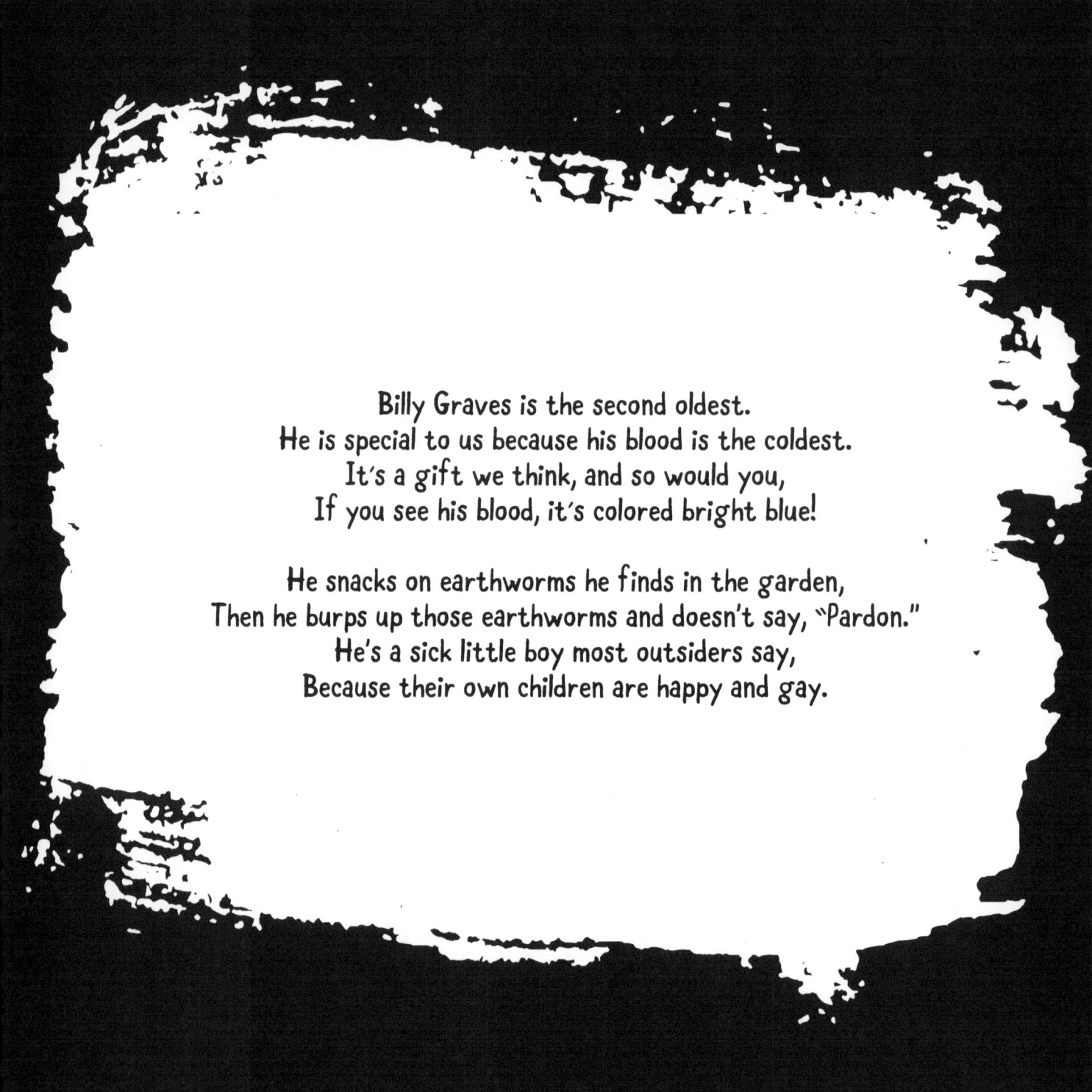

Billy Graves is the second oldest.
He is special to us because his blood is the coldest.
It's a gift we think, and so would you,
If you see his blood, it's colored bright blue!

He snacks on earthworms he finds in the garden,
Then he burps up those earthworms and doesn't say, "Pardon."
He's a sick little boy most outsiders say,
Because their own children are happy and gay.

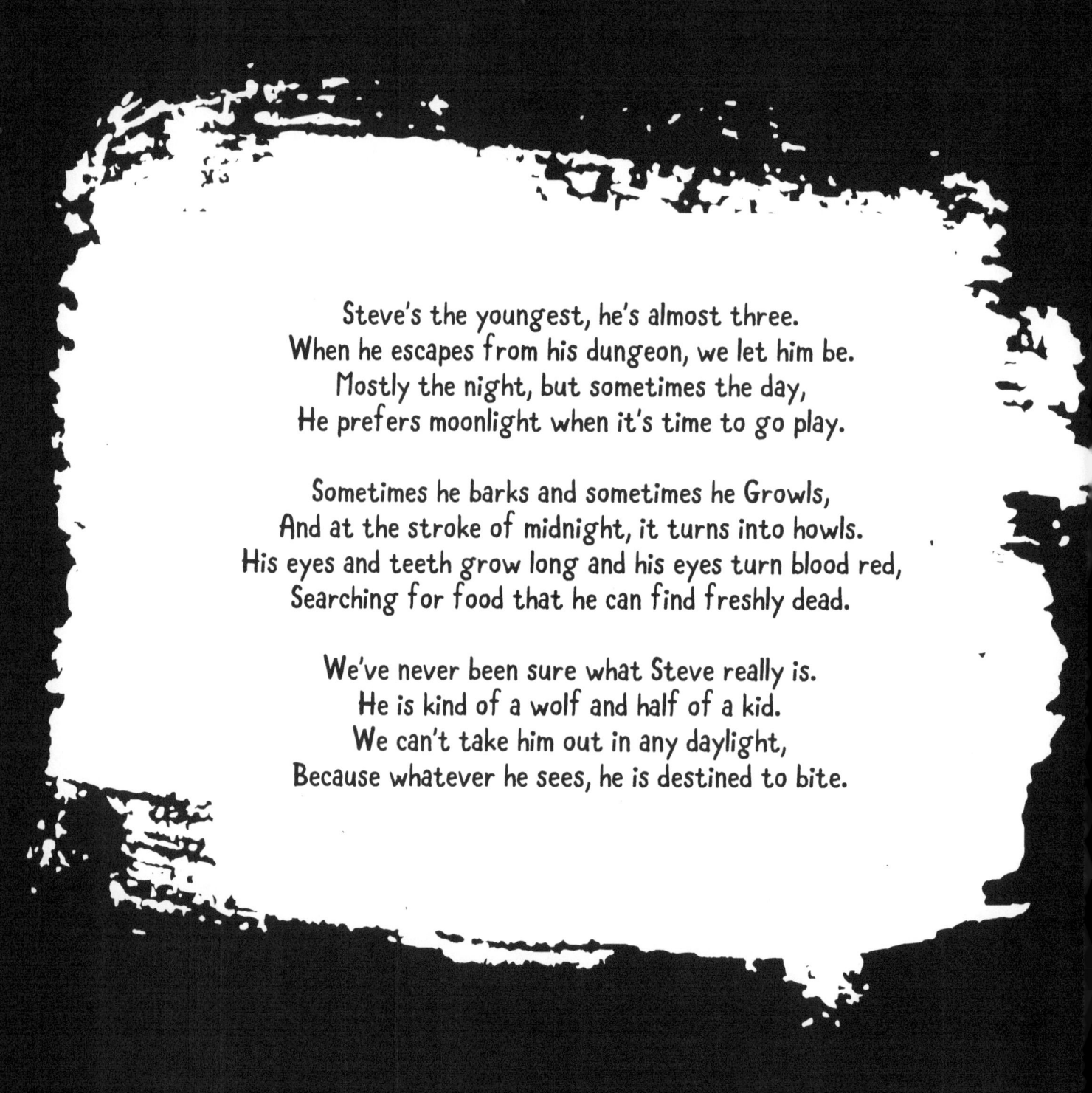

Steve's the youngest, he's almost three.
When he escapes from his dungeon, we let him be.
Mostly the night, but sometimes the day,
He prefers moonlight when it's time to go play.

Sometimes he barks and sometimes he Growls,
And at the stroke of midnight, it turns into howls.
His eyes and teeth grow long and his eyes turn blood red,
Searching for food that he can find freshly dead.

We've never been sure what Steve really is.
He is kind of a wolf and half of a kid.
We can't take him out in any daylight,
Because whatever he sees, he is destined to bite.

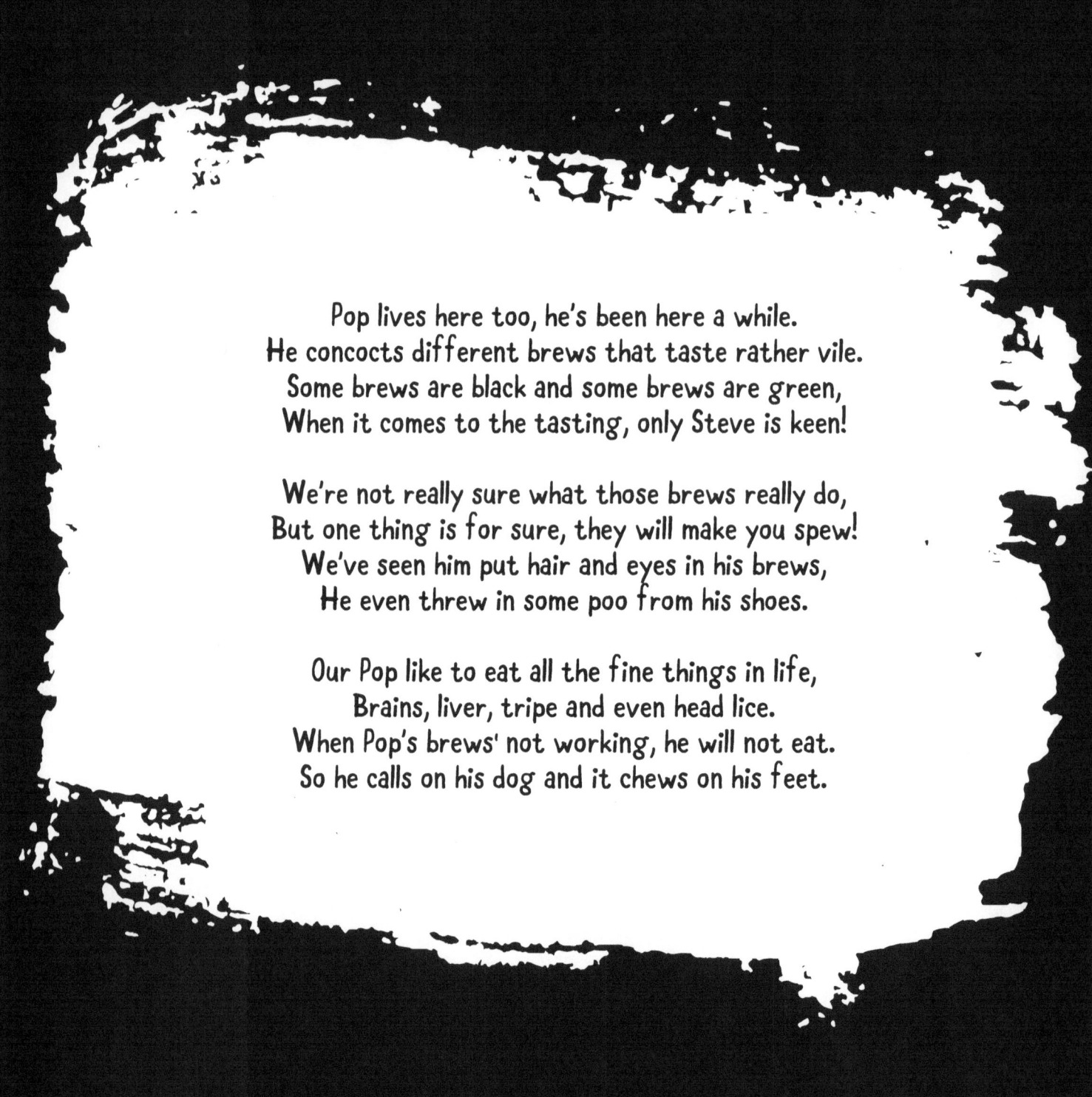

Pop lives here too, he's been here a while.
He concocts different brews that taste rather vile.
Some brews are black and some brews are green,
When it comes to the tasting, only Steve is keen!

We're not really sure what those brews really do,
But one thing is for sure, they will make you spew!
We've seen him put hair and eyes in his brews,
He even threw in some poo from his shoes.

Our Pop like to eat all the fine things in life,
Brains, liver, tripe and even head lice.
When Pop's brews' not working, he will not eat.
So he calls on his dog and it chews on his feet.

In the dark of the night, when the sun goes down,
Mum evolves into an evil clown.
Red hair, sharpened-teeth and an axe in her hand,
Scaring the things that pass by her land.

When the night turns to day and the sun comes up,
She mixes a potion in her chalice or cup.
Something that bubbles, fizzes or spews,
That usually smells like dirty old shoes.
She gulps it, and giggles in a cackling way,
It's the only way she will start her new day.

Our Dad is much stranger, he works quite a lot,
He mostly comes home all covered in snot.
His job is mainly to pick people's noses,
For compost for gardens to grow people's roses.

Dad likes to sleep in the graveyard at night,
He waits for some ghosts, to give them a fright.
The graveyard you see, is in our backyard,
So to spot one at night is never too hard.

But lurking behind that big, scary tree!
Something is happening, what can it be?
A rat, a ghoul or a breeze from the coast?
Dad screams and he runs, because it isn't a ghost.

By the light of the moon he sees an axe and big hair!
Not knowing it's Mum, she's always out there.
He never did know how Mum changed at night,
But Mum as a clown sure did give him a fright,
And all the ghosts giggled and laughed with delight.

The other one in our family is Nan,
She comes and visits whenever she can.
She is old and nice, much too sweet for us.
But boy, oh boy! Old Nan sure can cuss.
She has a white fluffy dog that she likes to call Peaches,
Deep down we all hope she'll be eaten by leeches.

Our great big, old python got out one day,
Eyeing off Peaches coming his way,
He waited and watched for the dog to go by,
Then he gulped her straight down in the blink of an eye.

We didn't tell Nan, because we knew she'd be sad,
When the snake did pass Peaches, we sure wished we had.
Nan saw little Peaches come out of the snake,
So she chopped off his tail with a sharp garden rake.

Now that sums us up, The Graves family.
As you can see, we're as sweet as can be!
A little bit quirky and sometimes not right,
Big deal if we hate the day and love night.
We hope to catch you again sometime,
For more spooky stories or even a rhyme.
Farewell from the Graves and all the pets too!

Bad dreams and worst luck from us to you.
Jacquelyne Lynn (aka Graves)